Disney
MULAN

AUTUMN
PUBLISHING

Long ago, the Great Wall kept China safe from invaders. But one dark night, the Hun army, led by the ruthless warrior Shan-Yu, stormed the wall.

Luckily, the Chinese Imperial Guard were able to light flaming cauldrons, sending out a warning of the attack to the people.

General Li reported back to the Imperial Palace, ready for battle.
But more soldiers were needed.

The Emperor ordered his counsel to go and call up recruits for the
Imperial Army. At least one man from every family would need to join.
"One man may be the difference between victory and defeat," he said.

Meanwhile, in a faraway village, a young Mulan was sat with her father, Fa Zhou, under a cherry blossom tree. Mulan was worried that she would never bring honour to her family.

Mulan's father pointed to one of the blooms. "This one's late," he said. "But when it blooms, it will be the most beautiful one of all."

Suddenly, they heard beating drums and horses' hooves.

A man from the Emperor's counsel announced that one man from every family must serve in the army. Knowing her father's injury, Mulan rushed forwards. "My father has already fought bravely," she said.

Her boldness outraged the Emperor's counsel. As Mulan's grandmother led her away, Fa Zhou received his conscription orders. But Mulan had a plan.

That night, as her family slept, Mulan cut off her hair, dressed in her father's armour and took his conscription papers. Women were forbidden to be soldiers, but Mulan was happy to risk her own life if it meant saving her father's. By the time her family woke up, Mulan and her horse, Khan, were long gone.

Frightened for her safety, they prayed to the Ancestors. They were going to send the Great Stone Dragon to guide Mulan, but after an accident, Mushu, a small dragon, had to go instead. He was joined by a lucky cricket called Cri-Kee.

Mushu and Cri-Kee reached Mulan just outside the army camp. "I have been sent by your ancestors to guide you," roared Mushu, as the glow of a campfire cast a large shadow of the tiny dragon.

Despite Mushu being little, Mulan was desperate for help and gladly accepted his offer. In the morning, she would report for duty.

The next morning, training began. Shang, the General's son, had been tasked with training the new recruits, including Mulan, who everyone believed was a man called Ping.

As part of the training, Shang shot an arrow to the top of a tall pole and his assistant, Chi Fu, then produced two heavy bronze discs. These were to be tied to the wrists of each trainee before they climbed the pole to retrieve the arrow. "One for discipline and one for strength," said Shang.

One after the other, each recruit tried to reach the arrow, but they all failed, including Mulan. Shang was less than impressed. Mulan, however, was not one to give up easily and she decided to try one last time. Putting a bronze disc on each wrist, she started to climb the pole... but kept sliding down.

Then, an idea came to her! Looping the weights together, she made a brace and hoisted herself all the way to the top. Everyone cheered!

Meanwhile, the Huns were advancing. Shan-Yu's falcon brought him a child's doll. From the doll's scent, Shan-Yu knew that it had come from the Tung-Shao Pass, where General Li's army was waiting. "The little girl will be missing her doll. We should return it," he said, sneering.

Back at camp, Mulan was enjoying a bath in a nearby lake when some of the other recruits jumped into the water. She had to get dressed before they discovered her secret! Mushu bit one of the recruits to create a distraction.

"Snake!" The frightened men jumped around while Mulan made her escape.

With Mulan's training going so well, Mushu began plotting to get her into the battle so she could become a hero. With Cri-Kee's help, he composed a letter ordering Shang to lead the recruits to the Tung-Shao Pass. They signed it from the General and made sure Shang saw it as soon as possible.

Led by Shang, the recruits arrived at the Pass, where they were quickly attacked by hundreds of Hun soldiers. "Prepare to fight," said Shang, bravely. "If we die, we die with honour."

As hordes of horsemen charged towards them, an idea spurred Mulan into action.

She grabbed a cannon and lit the fuse, firing it directly at the mountain. Snow came crashing down and smothered the advancing Huns, including an angry Shan-Yu, who just had time to slash at Mulan with his sword before being buried in the snow.

Mulan jumped on Khan's back and grabbed Shang just as the wall of snow pushed them over a cliff.

"Help!" Mulan called. She tied a rope around Khan, knotted the rope to her arrow and shot the arrow up to the soldiers, who managed to haul them to safety.

"Ping… I owe you my life," Shang said to Mulan.

As the recruits celebrated, Mulan realised she'd been hurt. The medic dressed the wound, but discovered she was a woman and revealed her secret to everyone.

Chi Fu charged Mulan with treason and ordered Shang to kill her.

As Mulan crouched down, Shang raised his sword, but then threw it down. Mulan had saved his, and everyone else's, life with her quick thinking.

"My debt is repaid," he said, then ordered they move on without her.

Mulan, Khan, Mushu and Cri-Kee huddled alone by a small fire.
Suddenly, there was a great howl. It was Shan-Yu! He was alive and heading towards the Emperor's palace. Mulan had to warn Shang, so she jumped on Khan and rode to the Imperial City as fast as possible.

When she arrived, a victory celebration was in full swing. Mulan quickly found Shang. "The Huns are alive!" she called. "They're in the city!"

Still feeling hurt and betrayed, Shang didn't believe her.

Just then, the Huns appeared and dragged the Emperor into the palace.

As the people panicked, Mulan came up with a plan and entered the palace to confront Shan-Yu. The pair fought furiously, ending up on the palace roof. Shan-Yu was angry and he lunged at Mulan, but she managed to pin his cloak to the roof. "Ready, Mushu?" asked Mulan.

Cri-Kee lit a fuse and Mushu, with a rocket attached to him, soared through the sky towards Shan-Yu.

The rocket hit the villain, tearing him free from his cloak and knocking him into the fireworks tower, causing an explosion. Shan-Yu had been defeated.

With the city saved, the Emperor approached Mulan. "I've heard a great deal about you, Fa Mulan," he said. "You stole your father's armour, impersonated a soldier, dishonoured the Chinese Army, destroyed my palace and... saved us all."

Then, to everyone's surprise, the Emperor bowed to Mulan.

Stunned, the crowd followed his example.

Back at home, Mulan embraced her father. "The greatest gift and honour is having you for a daughter," Fa Zhou said. "I've missed you so!"

Then, Shang arrived and everyone was delighted to welcome him into the Fa family home, especially Mulan.

With a little help from Mushu, Mulan had become a hero and a leader, bringing honour to her family in her own way.